Dear Parent:
Your child's love of reading starts here!

Every child learns to read in a different way and at his or her own speed. You can help your young reader improve and become more confident by encouraging his or her own interests and abilities. You can also guide your child's spiritual development by reading stories with biblical values and Bible stories, like I Can Read! books published by Zonderkidz. From books your child reads with you to the first books he or she reads alone, there are I Can Read! books for every stage of reading:

SHARED READING
Basic language, word repetition, and whimsical illustrations, ideal for sharing with your emergent reader.

BEGINNING READING
Short sentences, familiar words, and simple concepts for children eager to read on their own.

READING WITH HELP
Engaging stories, longer sentences, and language play for developing readers.

READING ALONE
Complex plots, challenging vocabulary, and high-interest topics for the independent reader.

ADVANCED READING
Short paragraphs, chapters, and exciting themes for the perfect bridge to chapter books.

I Can Read! books have introduced children to the joy of reading since 1957. Featuring award-winning authors and illustrators and a fabulous cast of beloved characters, I Can Read! books set the standard for beginning readers.

A lifetime of discovery begins with the magical words **"I Can Read!"**

Visit www.icanread.com for information on enriching your child's reading experience.
Visit www.zonderkidz.com for more Zonderkidz I Can Read! titles.

Command them to do good, to be rich in good
deeds, and to be generous and willing to share.
—*1 Timothy 6:18*

Jake Learns to Share
Text copyright © 2008 by Crystal Bowman
Illustrations copyright © 2008 by Karen Maizel

{story adapted from *Jonathan James Says "Happy Birthday to Me!"*
Chapter One—Jonathan's Birthday}

Requests for information should be addressed to:
Zonderkidz, Grand Rapids, Michigan 49530

Library of Congress Cataloging-in-Publication Data

Bowman, Crystal.
    Jake learns to share / by Crystal Bowman ; illustrated by Karen Maizel.
        p. cm. -- (Jake series) (I can read. Level 2)
      ISBN 978-0-310-71679-2 (softcover)
      [1. Sharing--Fiction. 2. Christian life--Fiction.] I. Maizel, Karen, ill. II. Title.
    PZ7.B68335Jail 2008
    [E]--dc22

                          2008008376

Art Direction and Design: Jody Langley

Printed in China

08 09 10 11 • 4 3 2 1

ZONDERkidz

I Can Read!™

READING 2 WITH HELP

Jake Learns to Share

story by Crystal Bowman

pictures by Karen Maizel

It was Jake's birthday.

Mother was making him a cake.

"May I lick the bowl?" asked Jake.

"Yes, you may," said Mother.

Jake licked the bowl.

Then he licked his fingers.

"I want my day to be very special.

I want to eat my whole cake

all by myself," said Jake.

"Are you sure?" asked Mother.

"Yes, I'm sure," said Jake.

"Well, okay then," said Mother.

"It is your birthday cake."

"Yes it is," said Jake.

Ding! Dong!

Grandma was at the door.

Jake let her in.

"Happy birthday," said Grandma.

"What did you get me?" asked Jake.

"You'll have to wait and see,"

said Grandma.

"I'm going to eat my whole cake
all by myself," said Jake.

"Oh, my," said Grandma.

"That's a lot of cake for one boy."

"Yes, it is," said Jake.

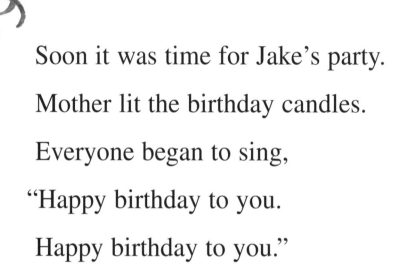

Soon it was time for Jake's party.

Mother lit the birthday candles.

Everyone began to sing,

"Happy birthday to you.

Happy birthday to you."

Jake blew out the candles.

"Did you make a wish?" asked Father.

"I wished for lots of presents,"
said Jake.

Then Jake ate his birthday cake.

Everyone watched him eat.

Jake ate three big pieces

all by himself.

"I'll have more later," he said.

"Now I want to open my presents!"

Jake opened all of his presents.

He got a baseball from Grandma

and a game from his sister, Kelly.

Mother and Father gave him

a new baseball mitt.

"I want to play with my presents,"

said Jake.

"Have fun," said Father.

Jake played with his presents

all by himself.

Jake threw his ball up in the air.

He caught it with his new mitt.

But Jake was not having fun.

Then Jake played with his new game.

But Jake still was not having fun.

Jake was sad.

"My birthday is no fun!" he cried.

"I think I know why," said Grandma.

"God wants you to share.

Sharing birthdays is much more fun."

Jake wiped his eyes.

"Will you play catch with me?"

asked Jake.

"Sure," said Grandma.

Grandma threw the ball to Jake.

Jake caught it in his new mitt.

"This is much more fun," he said.

"Will you play my new game with me?"

Jake asked Father.

"I would like that," said Father.

Jake and Father played his new game.

"This is much more fun," said Jake.

Then Jake saw his birthday cake.

"Let's have some cake," he said.

"Are you hungry?" asked Mother.

Jake shook his head.

"No, I'm not hungry," he said.

"I want to share my birthday cake."

Mother got plates for everyone.

Mother, Father, Grandma, and Kelly

all had some birthday cake.

Jake watched them eat.

"Thank you for all of my presents,"
 said Jake.

"You're welcome," said Mother.

"Did you have a fun birthday?"

"Oh, yes!" said Jake.

"I had fun playing catch
with Grandma.
And I had fun playing my new game
with Father."
"And we had fun eating your cake!"
said Kelly.

Jake smiled a great big smile.

"God wants us to share,"

he said.

"That's why birthdays are fun."